Jack's Bed

Lynne Rickards

Rosalind Beardshaw

Jessica
Evans Cla
fndsom

Green Bananas

EGMONT

We bring stories to life

First published in Great Britain 2007
by Egmont UK Ltd
239 Kensington High Street, London W8 6SA
Text copyright © Lynne Rickards 2006
Illustrations copyright © Rosalind Beardshaw 2006
The author and illustrator have asserted their moral rights.
ISBN 978 1 4052 2006 4
10 9 8 7 6 5 4 3
A CIP catalogue record for this title is available from the British Library.
Printed in Singapore.

I Don't Want to Go to Bed!

Staying in Bed

Imagine!

for Cameron

L.R.

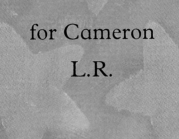

I Don't Want to Go to Bed!

'Bedtime train now leaving the station,' said Dad.

'I don't want to go to bed!' said Jack.

'Let's find those pyjamas,' said Mum.

'I don't want to go to bed!'

moaned Jack.

9

'Here's your toothbrush, Jack,'
said Mum.

'I dow wanna go a beh!'

spluttered Jack.

'There's still time for a story,'

suggested Dad.

Jack picked up his favourite books.

'Let's read these!' he said.

'Choose one!' laughed Mum. She
sat down next to him.

I like this story.

Jack snuggled close and looked
around the room.

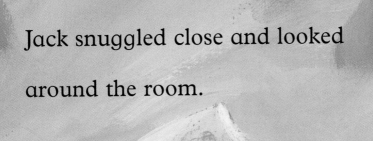

'What if there are monsters?'
worried Jack.

'I'll put on your night light,' said

Dad. 'That will scare them off.'

'We don't have monsters!' said Mum.

'Now, let's look at this book.'

'The little train went chug, chug, chug,' Mum began.

'I don't want to . . . go to . . . zzzzzzz,' snored Jack.

Staying in Bed

Jack woke up in the middle of the night. Everything was dark and quiet.

Jack saw strange shadows on the walls.

Was that a spiky monster beside the

bookcase?

He jumped up and went to Mum
and Dad's room. Their bed was
warm and cosy.

Jack felt much safer with Mum's
arm around him. No monsters could
get him now.

In the morning, Jack was back in his own bed. 'How did that happen?' he wondered.

At breakfast, Mum said, 'Today I think we'll get you a special stay-in-your-own-bed present.'

Jack was curious. A present for staying in his own bed? He wondered how long he might have to stay there.

Mum found some lovely furry animals. Inside each one was a hot water bottle. 'You choose,' said Mum.

Jack picked a spotty leopard. It had shiny amber eyes and wiry black whiskers.

At bedtime, Mum filled the leopard with hot water. It felt wonderfully warm and made a nice slooshy noise.

The leopard lay in Jack's lap while Dad read a story. Jack patted the soft, spotty fur.

Mum turned out the light and
tucked Jack in. 'Your leopard will
keep you safe and warm
tonight,' she smiled.

Jack snuggled down with his new
friend. He could see the leopard's
eyes sparkling, watching for monsters.

In the morning, Jack woke up with the leopard still curled up beside him. The stay-in-your-own-bed present had worked!

Imagine!

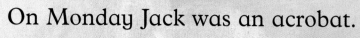

On Monday Jack was an acrobat.

He did fantastic flips on his
trampoline, bouncing as high as
the sky.

Whee!

On Tuesday Jack was a mountain climber, pulling on ropes to reach the highest snowy peak.

When he got to the top, he planted a
flag in the snow and had a picnic.

On Wednesday Jack took his

raft down a jungle river.

He used his paddle to whack

those pesky crocodiles.

On Thursday Jack explored a dark cave, crawling on his tummy like a snake.

When he found something for his
collection, he popped it into his pocket.

On Friday Jack decided

to build an igloo.

With the cold wind raging outside,

he was cosy and warm in his

Arctic house.

On Saturday Jack made an amazing tree house in the middle of the rainforest.

He invited a few friends over

for lunch.

On Sunday Jack took a long, hot
journey into the desert.

He rode a camel for miles and miles,
then parked him outside his tent for
the night.

After all his adventures, Jack was quite
tired out. Good night, Jack!